FOR HENRY

With love from your
1ST and 2nd grade teacher, Mrs. Cazet

The Shrunken Head

by Denys Cazet

Grandpa Spanielson's
CHICKEN POX STORIES
story #3

HarperCollins*Publishers*

Grandpa Spanielson's Chicken Pox Stories: Story #3: The Shrunken Head Copyright © 2007 by Denys Cazet All rights reserved.
Printed in the United States of America. No part of this book may be used or reproduced in any manner whatsoever without written
permission except in the case of brief quotations embodied in critical articles and reviews. For information address HarperCollins
Children's Books, a division of HarperCollins Publishers, 1350 Avenue of the Americas, New York, NY 10019.
www.harperchildrens.com

Library of Congress Cataloging-in-Publication Data
Cazet, Denys.
   The shrunken head / by Denys Cazet.— 1st ed.
      p.   cm.— (An I can read book) (Grandpa Spanielson's chicken pox stories ; story #3)
   Summary: As Barney continues to recover from the chicken pox, Grandpa tells him the story of how Dr. Storkmeyer's head was
shrunk during a jungle expedition.
   ISBN-10: 0-06-073013-7 (trade bdg.) — ISBN-13: 978-0-06-073013-0 (trade bdg.)
   ISBN-10: 0-06-073014-5 (lib. bdg.) — ISBN-13: 978-0-06-073014-7 (lib. bdg.)
   [1. Dogs—Fiction. 2. Storytelling—Fiction. 3. Chicken pox—Fiction. 4. Grandparents—Fiction. 5. Humorous stories—Fiction.]
I. Title. II. Series.
PZ7.C2985Shr 2006   2006000583
[E]—dc22

1 2 3 4 5 6 7 8 9 10   ❖   First Edition

For Mallory and Nate,
with much affection
—Uncle D.

Grandma tucked Barney into bed.

"My chicken pox itch," said Barney.

"I know," said Grandma.

"What this pup needs

is one of my famous anti-itch

Chicken Pox Stories!" said Grandpa.

"What this boy needs is rest,"
said Grandma. "Doctor Storkmeyer
will be coming by today."

"Doctor Storkmeyer!" said Grandpa.
"Ha! Did I ever tell you about
the time he got his head shrunk?"
"Wow!" said Barney. "Tell me!"

Grandma raised her right eyebrow.

"I'm going to the market," she said.

"Grandpa is going to mow the lawn.

Barney is going to take a nap."

"Grandpa's anti-itch stories

are better than a nap," said Barney.

Grandma kissed Barney.

"Later," she said. "I'll be back."

Grandpa watched Grandma

drive away in the pickup truck.

"Later," he mumbled.

"I'm too old for later!"

The doorbell rang.

It was Harold Piggerman,

Barney's friend from next door.

"Hi," said Harold.

"Here are some comic books for Barney."

Grandpa looked at Harold.

He looked at Grandma's candy jar

sitting by the door.

He grabbed a chocolate bar

and held it up.

"Can you read that?" he asked.

"No," said Harold.

"It's upside down."

"No, it isn't," said Grandpa.

"It's written in Piglish.

It was made in far away Pigland."

"Oh," said Harold.

"What does it say?"

"It says," said Grandpa,

"that whoever eats this candy bar

could grow up to be president

of a jelly donut factory

if he mows my lawn."

"Wow!" said Harold. "Want to trade?"

"Well . . . okay," said Grandpa.

"I'll get the mower," said Harold.

Grandpa walked back
to Barney's room.

Barney opened one eye.

"Hi," he said.

"Hi," said Grandpa. "Did you rest?"

"Sort of," said Barney.

"Did you mow the lawn?"

"Sort of," said Grandpa.

"How are you feeling?"

"Itchy," said Barney.

"Time for one of my famous
anti-itch stories!" said Grandpa.

The
Shrunken Head

Once upon a time,
in the olden days,
when grandmas
didn't drive pickup trucks,
I was a famous explorer.

One day,

Doc Storkmeyer and I

were riding our bicycles

in the jungle.

We heard something strange.

"What is that?" asked Doc.

"Drums," I said. "Headhunter drums!
This is Pooch country."
Suddenly, poison arrows shot out
of the jungle and stuck in our tires.

The Pooches surrounded us.

They carried us to their village.

They danced around us for hours

making rude remarks.

Then the drums stopped.

The Pooches fell to their knees.

"The queen! The queen!" they cried.

"Queen Peekatmyknees!"

The queen smiled at me.

"I love you, handsome one," she said.

"You will be my king.

We will have many puppies."

"Never!" I shouted.

"Very well," said the queen.

"Use the shrink juice!"

The Pooches picked up Doc

and held him above the juice.

"Last chance!" said the queen.

"Never!" I said.

"Dip the duck!" cried the queen.

The Pooches dipped Doc into the juice.

"What is that stuff?" I asked.

"Triple-sour lemonade

and cranberry juice!" said the queen.

"Now will you be my king?"

asked the queen.

"No!" I said. "Never!"

"Dip the duck!" she shouted.

"We've got to get out of here,"

I whispered.

"You're telling me!" said Doc.

"RUN!" I shouted.

I pushed over the shrink juice.

The Pooches slipped and slid

and fell into the juice.

They screamed as they shrunk.

Their spears became toothpicks.

"Stop them!" cried the queen.

They chased us into the jungle.

We ran to our bicycles.

I grabbed the bicycle pump

and screwed the hose

into Doc's bellybutton.

I pumped and pumped.

His head got bigger and bigger.

Just a tad more!

"Too much!" he cried.

I let out some air.

"Better!" he squeaked.

A tiny spear whizzed by.

"There they are!" I yelled.

Poison darts shot past us.

The Pooches grabbed one bicycle.

I grabbed the other.

Doc climbed onto my shoulders.

"Go! Go!" he cried.

Faster, faster.

We rode that bicycle on flat tires

all the way out of the jungle

and all the way home.

"Wow," said Barney. "It's lucky you—"

"Anybody home?"

Doctor Storkmeyer called.

"In here," shouted Grandpa.

Doctor Storkmeyer

peeked into Barney's room.

"There you are," he said.

"Try not to stare at his head,"

Grandpa whispered.

Barney stared at his head.

"How's my favorite patient?"

asked Doctor Storkmeyer.

"What?" said Barney.

"The itches," said Doctor Storkmeyer.

"It looks like they're drying up."

"It's Grandpa's anti-itch stories,"

said Barney.

"I'm sure," said Doctor Storkmeyer.

"I've heard those stories for years.

They'd dry up anything."

"At least they're free," said Grandpa.

"I'm home," called Grandma.

She carried a tray into the bedroom.

"Cold drinks," she said.

"Lemonade and cranberry juice."

"I'll try a little of each,"
said Doctor Storkmeyer.
Grandpa looked at Barney.
"Uh-oh," said Barney.